Obi And His Next Curious Adventures

Written by Chinasa Uyanna

Illustrated by Troy Edwards

Ikenga Publishing Ltd

Ikenga Publishing Ltd would like to thank Sarah Khan, Vicky Garrard, Ngozi Okoyeze and Ada Maya Uyanna-Diaz for their contribution in helping the book reach release phase.

This book is set way back in the 1980s, which was before most people had the internet, smartphones and tablets. Throughout the book you may see and read things which are very different to what life is like nowadays.

Obi has lived in London, United Kingdom, for most of his life but, seven months ago, he came to stay with his grandma in Nimo, Anambra State, Nigeria. He is now five years and one month old, and has started picking up some of the local language and sayings.

He quickly became used to wearing sandals, t-shirts and shorts during the hot summer season and to hiding away indoors during the rainy season.
Now it is late December, which is the sunny season in Nimo.

Obi said 'Grandma, what is that, is it a monster?'
Grandma laughed and said, 'There are no monsters
here, it's a masquerade. There are many different
masquerades in Nigeria depending on tribes, however
the one you are looking at is an Igbo masquerade,
called Mmanwu.'

'Emmm-mann-woo,' said Obi, trying to repeat the name. Grandma responded, 'It is difficult to pronounce just from looking at the word, but you said it correctly.'

Masquerades are popular during festive periods like Christmas and Easter. Masqueraders usually perform a dance or a short drama scene and that is a form of entertainment for local people. They symbolise a new set of months to come; a new season.

Obi went with his grandma in her pick-up truck to a nearby farm. Grandma had developed a number of partnerships with local farmers that produced fresh food products to be sold in the markets. She greeted one of the leading farmers "Kedu" and the farmer responded "Odinma"

Obi interrupted and asked, 'What are we doing here?'
'We are going to barter with these farmers, and hopefully get a good price for some of the lovely vegetables that you see here, in order to sell to the market traders. I act as the person who buys from the farmers and sells to the market traders, what we call a "broker".'

Obi was worried; did Grandma say she was 'broken'? She looked fine to him.

Grandma arrived at the markets and began delivering some of the goods to the traders who sold the vegetables or fruits to local customers.

Obi saw, in some cases, Grandma receiving large amounts of money and, in some cases, she just said "Let's settle next month" to the market traders.
Obi realised that a broken person was someone who received money after delivering something.

Later in the day Grandma corrected Obi, 'I am not "broken" but a "broker".' She also taught him some basic sums to help him understand about the currency in Nigeria, which was called Naira.

'Today class we are going to learn mathematics by using small sums of money to do some simple adding and subtracting,'
Mrs Okoye said to the class.

Mrs Okoye taught children aged 5 and 6 at the local school Obi attended. 'Should we start with you Obi?

I am guessing you must be used to Naira now. What is 3+3, and then what is 4+4? Think of receiving Naira as you respond, ok?' Obi replied, 'The first answer is 6 Naira, and the second answer is 8 Naira.'

'That is correct,' said Mrs Okoye 'Have you been practising equations at home?'

Obi said, 'Yes, my grandma has been teaching me as she is involved in the markets. She even taught me subtractions like 10-5, which is 5.'

Mrs Okoye said, 'Your grandma has taught you well, you are lucky to learn about the markets.'

Obi met his cousin Chika in the playground and noted that some children were playing a game that he had never seen before. Obi said 'What is the name of this game you are playing?'

'It is called the Oga game', Chika responded. 'The game is played by two or more of us clapping hands and placing a foot forward. Why don't you watch us and perhaps you can join in when you feel confident, ok?'

Obi replied 'Ee Biko', which means 'yes please', in Igbo.
Obi joined in later, but found it difficult to get used to the game.
I need more practice, he thought.

Uncle Peter came to visit the family and spent a few days at Grandma's house. He had not seen Obi since picking him up from the airport when he first arrived.

Uncle Peter said, 'Obi, can we still call you "London boy"?'

Obi responded, 'Perhaps you can call me "Londonimo boy".'
Uncle Peter laughed. 'Have you joined two cities together
to form one?'
'*Ee*,' said Obi,
which meant "yes" in Igbo.

Can you identify two
items from the
markets on the
table?

While lying in bed, some memories came back to Obi of London and he wondered what might have changed since he left. Grandma told him during dinner that he would likely return to London when he was six.

Obi was excited about this but was also glad that it was not any time soon. He wanted to get better at the Oga game with Chika's help and spend more time in the markets.

THE END......OR UNTIL THE LAST CURIOUS ADVENTURE........

Let's check how well you know Obi and his curious adventures. READY for some questions?

QUESTIONS
1. How old is Obi?
2. What seasons were described at the beginning of the book?
3. At what times of the year do local people see masquerades?
4. What is grown in the farmland by farmers?
5. What is the currency used in Nigeria called?

Let's check how well you know Obi and his curious adventures. READY for some questions?

QUESTIONS
6. What sums did Mrs Okoye ask Obi to do in the classroom?
7. Who taught Obi how to add and subtract?
8. What was the name of the game that Chika played in the playground?
9. What was the name of the uncle that visited Grandma's house?
10. How old will Obi be when he returns to London?

Ikenga Publishing Ltd is a small London based boutique publisher specialising in the production of creative works that references West African culture.

Text © Chinasa Uyanna. Illustrations © Troy Edwards
First published in UK in 2021 by Ikenga Publishing Ltd

20-22 Wenlock Road, London, England, N1 7GU

ISBN: 978-1-3999-0261-8

The illustrations was created in watercolour and then edited digitally.

Manufactured in UK.